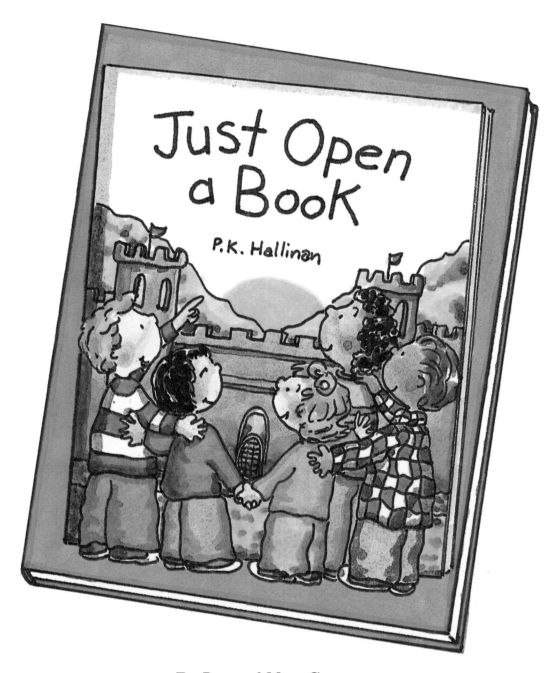

*For Ben and Mary Courson,
two of my favorite readers.*

Ideals Children's Books • Nashville, Tennessee
an imprint of Hambleton-Hill Publishing, Inc.

Published by Ideals Children's Books
An imprint of Hambleton-Hill Publishing, Inc.
Nashville, Tennessee 37218

Printed and bound in the United States of America

Library of Congress Cataloging-in-Publication Data

Hallinan, P.K.
    Just open a book / written and illustrated by P.K. Hallinan.
        p.   cm.
    Summary: Rhymed text and illustrations describe the many adventures
one can find in books.
    ISBN 1-57102-139-6 (hardcover) ISBN 1-57102-015-2 (pbk.)
    [1. Books and reading—Fiction. 2. Stories in rhyme.] I. Title.
    PZ8.3.H15Jv   1995
    [E]—dc20   93-31994
                                                                CIP
                                                                AC

Just open a book
and begin to read through
the world of enjoyment
that's waiting for you.

You can take a long trip
on an old pirate ship,

or walk in the sand
where the pyramids stand.

You can go to the moon
and then, if you please,
you can see for yourself
if it's made of green cheese.

Just open a book—
it's all you need do
to make your most fabulous
wishes come true.

So next time you think
you've got nothing to do,
just look at the books
that were written for you.

or even to cook.
It's easy if you'll . . .